WELCOME TO
YOUR *AMAZING* adventures™

Inside awaits an adventure that only you can have. It takes place in faraway, long ago lands. Monsters, sorcerers, and evil kings may oppose you, but you have the power to outwit them all. Your skill at pathfinding can steer you through all the perils, natural and otherwise, that stand in your path. If you are a good explorer of the mazes that block your journey, you'll win through in the end.

And if you get caught in the pitfalls of a maze, you can retrace your steps and try to find a better way out. That way, your skill determines the outcome.

You can be the hero, and save the kingdom from the evil forces that threaten it.

If you're ready to go for it, turn the page and see what challenges await you.

Good luck!

YOUR **AMAZING** adventures™ #3

TERROR UNDER THE EARTH

by
Richard Brightfield

Illustrated by Paul Abrams

TOR

A TOM DOHERTY ASSOCIATES BOOK

Copyright © 1984 by Richard Brightfield
Cover art and interior illustrations copyright © 1984 by Paul and Karen Abrams
Mazes copyright © 1984 by Richard and Glory Brightfield
YOUR AMAZING ADVENTURES™ is a trademark of Richard Brightfield

A Tor Book, published by arrangement with Bluejay Books Inc.

Published by Tom Doherty Associates, 8-10 W. 36th Street, New York, New York 10018

A Bluejay Books Production

First printing, December 1984

ISBN: 0-812-56040-X
CANADIAN ISBN: 0-812-56041-8

Printed in the United States of America

ATTENTION!

You are about to enter an exciting world of sword and sorcery. *You* are the hero or heroine. You will have many adventures and face many dangers, but be especially careful going through the mazes—a wrong turn may be your last.

Once you have started on a path inside a maze, DON'T GO BACK—unless you reach a dead end. Finally, you will either get through the maze or enter a trap. Turn to the page indicated to discover your fate.

You are an adventurer. With your two friends, Teppin and Aran, you have explored the islands of the Western Sea as well as the many lands of Arcanthia. At the moment, you are on the small ship that the three of you share. You are on your way back to the walled city of Trangor on the Dracan coast after returning the young girl, Tana, to her own land. You had rescued her from the Island of Fear.

Your landfall is far to the north of Trangor. It is a coast that you've heard many stories about, not all of them good. You've never actually sailed along it before.

"The land yonder," Teppin says, pointing to the coast, "is one that was long ravaged by wars. Some say that all of the inhabitants that were not killed left the land and settled elsewhere, though no one seems to know just where."

"I've heard those stories too," Aran says. "We'd better give it a wide berth."

"I wish we could," Teppin says, "but we're low on drinking water. We don't know how many days it will take us to get south to Trangor."

"That coast looks pretty barren to me," you say. "We'll be lucky if we find anything there."

"Look!" Aran shouts. "Doesn't that look

like a break in the hills. It could be where a river empties into the sea. Maybe if we sail inland...."

"A good idea," Teppin says. "We'll head for it and see what it is."

As you get closer to shore, you see that the coast is made up of high, rugged cliffs. Off in the distance to the right is what looks like the cone of a fire mountain, though no smoke is coming from it. The land above the cliffs looks flat and for the most part treeless.

"That definitely is an inlet of the sea," Aran says. "I can see it clearly now. It leads into a fjord."

Soon you are at the foot of the towering cliffs, looking all the more desolate and foreboding close up. There is no beach. The waves from the sea break against the bottom of the cliffs themselves.

As you sail in through the inlet, a towering natural sea gate, you feel the strong pull of the tide surging into the fjord.

"This is going to be easy," you say. "All we have to do is steer and the tide will do the rest."

"Aye, the tide is strong," Teppin says. "A bit too strong for *my* liking."

Your ship races along the base of the cliff inside the fjord. Then you see that you are heading for some sort of disturbance in the water.

"What's that up ahead!" Aran shouts.

"It looks like a whirlpool," Teppin says.

"Oh, my! What are we going to do!" you exclaim.

"The main thing is not to panic," Teppin says. "In my pirating days, I came across many of these whirlpools. Don't try to steer directly away from it or it will just pull you toward the center. There you'll be sucked down into the deep."

Go to next page.

"How do I steer then?" you ask.

"Go with the spinning current," Teppin says, "but always steer slightly to the outside."

"I sure hope you're right," Aran says. "If not, well, goodby us!"

Moments later, the ship is caught in the outer part of the whirlpool. It is whirled around in a wide circle. You follow Teppin's advice and let the ship go with the current. This seems to work for awhile, but then you feel the ship being slowly drawn toward the center.

Suddenly, you hear someone shouting in the water. Then you see a head bobbing up and down not far away. It's being carried along by the current the same as you are.

"There's somebody out there!" you shout to Teppin. "See if you can throw him a line."

Teppin jumps to the rail and tosses out the bow rope toward the struggling figure. He grabs at it desperately, but can't quite reach it.

Fortunately, the figure is being carried along on a parallel course with the ship. Teppin pulls in the rope and throws again. This time it falls right across the bobbing head. The figure manages to grab it.

"Hold on!" you shout.

Teppin and Aran pull him toward the ship. When he is close enough, Teppin slips down the rope into the water and grabs— one arm under the shoulders of the figure and one arm holding the rope. Aran reaches down to help pull whoever it is aboard while Teppin follows, climbing back up the rope.

All this time, you are holding onto the tiller, trying to steer the ship out of the whirlpool. You are doing your best, but it's a tricky operation. Sometimes you manage to work your way further away from the center. Other times you are pulled you toward it.

Go to next page.

Find your way through the whirlpool maze. Be careful. If you get drawn into the vortex, you'll be sucked down into the sea. And remember what it says on page 5.

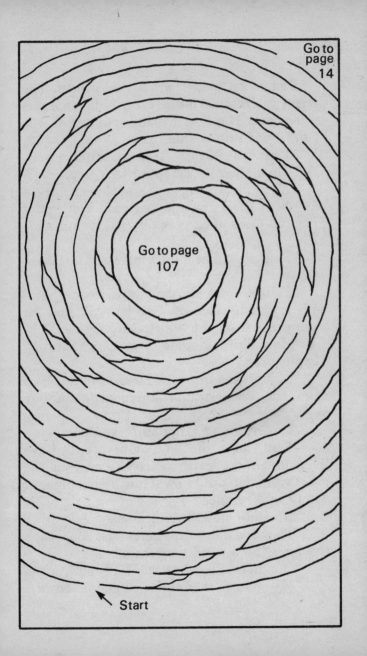

Go to
page
14

Go to page
107

Start

You've escaped from the whirlpool. The person you rescued is still lying half-conscious on the deck. The ship is drifting off to the side of the fjord into a small cove.

"That was close!" Aran exclaims.

"Good steering," Teppin tells you.

The figure on the deck starts to stir. It's a boy about the same age as Aran. You find a rolled up piece of canvas and put it under his head.

"That should be a little more comfortable," you say.

"Thank you," the boy says weakly, and with a strange accent. "And thank you for saving me from the whirlpool."

"How did you come to be caught in it?" Teppin asks.

"I blundered into it as I was swimming up from the underground kingdom," the boy says.

"Underground kingdom?" you say.

"Yes," says the boy. "Our people have lived under the earth since the time of the great wars. Up until now it has been a place of safety and refuge."

"Up until now?" Aran asks.

"That is a story that I must tell you," says the boy, "for I need your help."

"Our help? In what way?" Teppin asks.

"My name is Fendar—Fendar Kran,"

says the boy. "I am a prince of the royal family of Zanicor, our name for the underground kingdom. My uncle, Sline Kran, has usurped the throne and declared himself emperor. He has imprisoned the rest of my family—even worse, he has turned them into vords along with most of my people. Only I, and a few others, have managed to escape."

"Vords?" you ask. "What are those?"

Go to next page.

"Mindless creatures," Fendar says, "that are forced to obey his every command. Sline has started a reign of terror under the earth. He has somehow released the zarks from their long sleep and is using them not only to enslave us but to prepare an army that will someday attack the countries on the surface—up here!"

"Vords? Zarks?" Aran says. "Whatever

they are it doesn't sound too good."

"There must be something that can be done," you say.

"If you could come back with me, then maybe...," Fendar starts.

"And leave the ship!" Teppin exclaims.

"We could anchor it in this cove," you say, "and go take a look with Fendar."

"How do we get there?" Aran asks.

"The entrance is through an underwater cavern," Fendar says.

"How can we swim that far under water?" Teppin asks. "We're not fish."

"Don't worry," Fedar says. "As soon as you get through the underwater entrance there will be air enough to breathe."

"If you say so," says Teppin. "But I'm not sure how much help we can be. This Slime, or whatever his name is, seems to have things pretty well sewed up."

"There are those who are resisting," Fendar says. "But they need some new ideas. There has been nothing but peace under the earth for many years and they have forgotten how to fight. That's why we need someone from the surface to lead us."

"How far away is this entrance?" you ask.

Fendar stands up and goes to the rail of the ship. He stares intently down into the clear water, his hand shielding his eyes from the light. "I'm fairly sure it's right over there, not far below the surface of the water," he says. "You'll have to forgive me, this is my first time to the surface world and—"

"The first time on the surface!" Aran exclaims. "Really?"

"Yes," Fendar replies. "I was born in Zanicor and raised there. We have heard such horrible stories about the surface people that we have always been afraid to come up here. But now that our kingdom is beset by even more terrible things. . . ."

"All right, then," Teppin says. "Let's take a look down there. The ship is anchored firmly enough."

Fendar is the first to dive. You are next. You can see Fendar through the clear water swimming a short distance ahead. Teppin and Aran follow behind you.

Go to next page.

Fendar swims deeper, and almost immediately you can see an opening, a dark circle in the rock. Fendar disappears into it and you follow. You hope there's not far to go, you don't know how much longer your breath will hold out. There's less light in the underwater tunnel, but you can still see Fendar's shape up ahead. He's moving slightly upward now. Your air is about gone and you are starting to get dizzy.

Then suddenly, you break the surface of an underground lake. Teppin and Aran appear soon afterward. All of you are gasping for breath. You are inside a large cavern. There is a pale light coming from somewhere. You all swim toward the shore of the small lake.

Go to next page.

"This place is strange," you say, "with all those stone spears hanging from the ceiling."

"Not to mention the ones rising from the floor," Aran adds.

"I think the water slowly dripping down from above makes them in some way," Fendar says, "though I'm not exactly sure how. Lately there have been terrible tremors here under the ground. Many of the stone spears have been shaken down. Some of the passageways have even collapsed."

"As if we didn't have enough problems...," Aran says.

"Right now our problem is," Teppin says, "where do we go from here?"

"We have to try and find our way back through the maze of caverns to where the few that have escaped from Sline are hiding."

"Well... ah, I don't know this part of the kingdom that well," Fendar says. "I *did* find my way to this lake which I had always heard was a way to the upper world. I'm sure that I can find the way back."

"All right, then," says Teppin, "let's get going."

With Fendar leading, you all start into the cavern, winding your way around the many stone spears rising from the floor. Fendar, though, still seems confused about which way to go.

Suddenly, he rushes foward. "It's this way, I know it!" he exclaims.

"Hey! Fendar!" you shout. "Wait for us. Don't get too far ahead. I can barely see you in this dim light."

But Fendar has vanished into the gloom up ahead. You hurry after him, but the forest of spears makes the going difficult.

Then you hear what sounds like a cry far ahead in the tunnel. You all stop for a moment and listen.

Go to next page.

"Fendar! Are you all right up there?"
Aran calls out, his voice reverberating in the
cavern.

"I don't like this a bit," Teppin says.
"Best we get back to the boat and forget
about this whole thing. It may be that this
Fendar is leading us into a trap."

"You may be right," you say, "but let's
wait for awhile and see. He might come back

when he realizes that we're not following him."

"And we can use the rest," says Aran.

You all sit down on the damp floor, your backs against the stone pillars. You wait for what seems like about an hour.

"I guess we'd better start back," you say. "Too bad about Fendar, but—"

Suddenly, there is a deep rumbling and the floor of the cavern starts to shake. Some of the overhead spears break loose and come crashing down around you. Fortunately, none of them hit you or your friends. But seconds later, there is a tremendous roar in the tunnel that leads back to the small lake where you came in. That whole section of cavern collapses, sealing off the route back to your boat.

Then, there is silence again.

"Now we've had it," Aran exclaims. "We're sealed into this cavern."

"The way ahead doesn't seem to be too badly affected," you say. "I guess we have no choice but to go forward and find our way through."

Go to next page.

Find your way through the cavern maze. But be careful. You don't know what happened to Fendar. Whatever did happen, the same thing could happen to you.

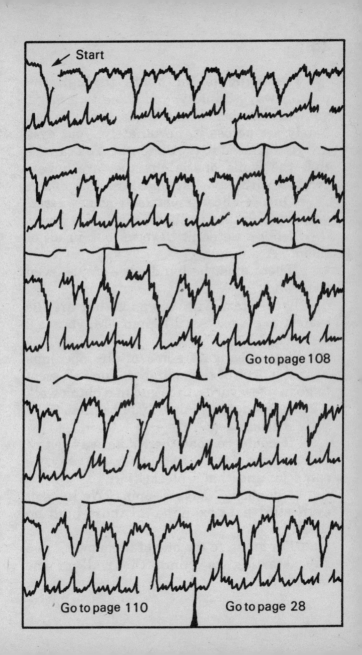

Start

Go to page 108

Go to page 110

Go to page 28

You struggle for hours through the passageways. Finally, you come to a large, vaulted chamber. It is so wide, that you can barely see across it. Fortunately, your eyes are getting used to the dim light. You can see that the walls of the chamber are honey-combed with cave-like openings.

"One of those must lead somewhere," you say pointing to them.

"I hope we don't have to look in all of them," Aran says.

"There must be hundreds—maybe even thousands."

"We'll start with the ones that are the easiest to get to," says Teppin. "Maybe we'll get lucky."

You investigate some of the openings near the floor of the chamber. They all seem to go in a few yards, then end in a blank wall. After a few dozen of them, you begin to feel a little discouraged.

"It could be that there's *no* way out of here," Aran says. "Except for the way we came in, and that's blocked off."

"I doubt it," says Teppin. "We haven't even started to examine all those high up there."

"I'm going to try one of them next," you say, starting to climb the wall of the chamber.

"Good idea," Teppin says. "I'll be right behind you."

The wall is fairly easy to climb. It has a lot of jagged edges that provide good footholds. You pull yourself up carefully.

You are about halfway up to your goal— an opening that resembles a man-made arched doorway—whan a large rock comes bouncing down from above, heading in your direction.

Go to next page.

"What the—" you start, as you pull yourself quickly to one side to escape the rock.

Aran lets out a yell of alarm below and Teppin mutters a few choice curses, no doubt remembered from his pirate days. But fortunately, the rock misses all of you. You hang there for a few moments before starting upwards again.

"Don't come any further," a shrill, high voice calls out from above, "or next time I won't miss."

"Hold it!" you call out. "We're friends of Prince Fendar. We came down from the land above. We're here to try to help the underground people."

"You are?" the voice asks in a milder tone.

A small, wizened head appears for a moment, peering over the ledge above. "Well, you don't look like zarks, or even vords. Come ahead then, but don't try anything. I still have some tricks up my sleeve."

You, Aran, and Teppin climb the rest of the way up to the ledge where the head had appeared. As you reach it, you see a small figure retreating back into the depths of one of the caves. You follow him.

You find yourselves in a brightly lit room surrounded by bottles and vials of all different sizes. They are all filled with different colored liquids.

"This is my laboratory," says the figure. "My name is Vankon and I was the royal alchemist before that wretched Sline took over. I'm no longer trying to find how to turn lead into gold, I'm trying to find an antidote to trope, the poison that Sline is using to turn people into vords."

Go to next page.

"Trope?" you say.

"Yes," says Vankon, "The foul liquid that Sline forces them to drink."

"How did he get your people to take this trope in the first place," Aran asks.

"First he roused the evil, horrible-looking zarks from their long slumber deep in the earth," says Vankon. "I think he uses the same substance to keep them awake. I'm not sure about that, but..."

Go to next page.

Vankon seems to drift off into deep thought for a few moments.

"Have you had any luck with this anti... anti...," starts Teppin.

"—Dote, anti-dote," says Vankon. "It can destroy the trope and make it harmless. At least I hope it can. I haven't been able to test it. That is, I haven't been able to get through to the vords to try it out. There are zarks everywhere, and they have orders to kill me on sight. And I must continue working here until I am sure."

"Where are the vords?" Teppin asks.

"Sline keeps them beyond the Scintari River, the underground river that flows through our kingdom, or what *was* our kingdom before Sline seized power," Vankon says.

"If we could get there, maybe we could try out the antidote for you," you say.

"It is so dangerous," says Vankon. "I can hardly ask it."

"Just give us some of this stuff and tell us how to get there," says Teppin.

"Oh, thank you," says Vankon. "No matter what happens, the kingdom will always be grateful."

Vankon hands Teppin a small, sealed bottle of powder which Teppin tucks away in his belt.

"There is only one way from here to the river, and that is through a maze of jagged passageways," says Vankon. "Be careful though. The edges of the rock are very sharp. I will lead you to the entrance. Oh, and here is another vial, one that will help light your way. When the light dims, just shake it."

You take the light-vial. It has a cord that allows you to hang it around your neck. Then you all follow Vankon as he leads you to an opening all the way at the top of the outside chamber. You, Teppin, and Aran climb through.

Go to next page.

Find your way through the jagged maze to the river.

Go to page
38

Go to page
109

Start

As you find your way through the jagged maze, you begin to hear a low, roaring sound. Sometimes it's louder, sometimes it's softer.

"That sound must be the river," you say.

"I think it is," Teppin says. "We'll try to head for it."

Finally, you find one passageway where the sound is *very* loud. You follow it to the end. Suddenly, you come out onto a narrow platform jutting out into a broad, rushing stream. You shake the vial hanging around your neck. There is a burst of light, then it settles down to a duller glow. But for a moment, the high, vaulted cavern through which the river runs is lit up. You see the water rushing by and you get a glimpse of a continuous ledge running the length of the opposite bank. The ledge you are on now only runs a short way up and down the stream, and then vanishes back into the vertical walls of the cavern.

"The river is flowing pretty fast," Aran shouts above the noise of the water. "If we swim across, we're going to end up far downstream."

"I know, but it looks like there's no other way," Teppin shouts back. The main thing is not to get separated in that current."

"Let's all hold onto my whip," you shout, unfastening it from your belt.

"Good idea!" Teppin shouts.

You unroll your whip. You hold onto the handle while Teppin grabs the end with Aran in the middle. Then you all count to three and jump into the swiftly flowing current.

Go to next page.

It seems like forever before you get to the other bank. You can't tell how far downstream you've gone except that you know you've gone a long way. Fortunately, the ledge is only inches above the water—you don't have much strength left to pull yourself up and out. You all sit there for awhile, panting and gasping for breath.

The sound of the water is quieter where you are now.

"Where do we go from here?" Aran asks.

"I'm not sure," you say, "We—"

Suddenly, in the dim light, you are aware of dozens of dark forms—on both sides of you.

"I'm afraid we're not alone," you whisper to Teppin. "Give that light-bottle of yours a shake and let's see what we're up against," Teppin says.

You do. In the bright flash that follows, you see an array of horrible creatures, their eyes glowing with fire in the brief light. You all jump to your feet and prepare to defend yourselves. Aran gets his slingshot ready while Teppin holds his knife in front of him. You, of course, have your whip.

"They must be zarks," you say. "They certainly fit the description that Vankon gave us."

Before you can say anything else, one of

the zarks charges toward you, a sword in one hand and a spear in the other. You strike with your whip, catching the zark around the knees. He goes sprawling on the slippery ledge, at the same time dropping his spear. Then he goes sailing off the ledge, into the stream, and in another second, is carried away by the current. Aran reaches down and scoops up the fallen spear to use as an extra weapon.

Go to next page.

There is an angry murmuring among the other zarks as they start to close in. You, Aran, and Teppin stand with your backs to the wall, waiting for the attack. You snap your whip in the air a few times. Its loud,

creacking sound seems to puzzle the zarks
and they stop where they are for a moment.

In the brief silence that follows, you hear
a sound like rushing air just over your head.
You look up. In the dim light you can just

make out an opening up on the wall. Teppin and Aran see it too.

"I don't know what's through that hole," you say, "but it can't be much worse than what's on this side."

"Quick then!" Teppin exclaims, "let's get up there."

Teppin gives you a lift up with his hands and you dive through the hole. Turning quickly inside, you lower your whip for Teppin and Aran to climb up. Before the zarks can fully react, the three of you are through the hole and inside some sort of chamber. Aran props the spear up against the inside wall so that the point sticks into the opening.

"This may stop them for a bit," he says.

You shake the vial hanging around your neck to get more light.

"Looks like these walls are made of mud—soft mud," Teppin says. "And there's a passageway leading off there."

You stand there watching the hole you just came through. The zarks don't seem to be following you. In fact, you can hear their angry grunts fading off down along the stream outside.

"Do you think we should go back out to the river?" Aran asks.

"No," says Teppin. "The zarks may be

trying to lure us out. It might be better to see where this passageway goes."

You go down the passageway. Soon you realize that you are in a maze, a maze carved in mud.

Go to next page.

Find your way through the mud maze. But be careful. The mud may have dangers all its own.

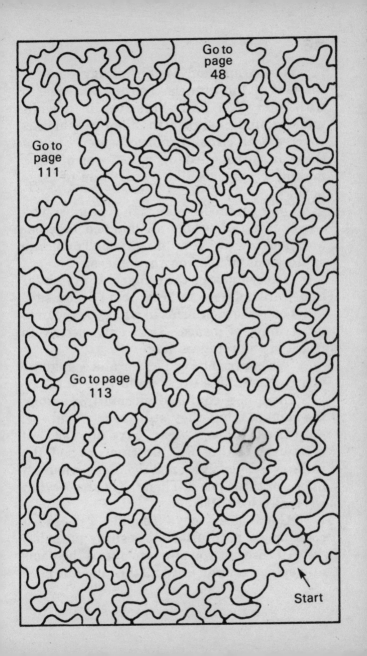

Go to
page
48

Go to
page
111

Go to page
113

Start

You, Aran, and Teppin struggle out of the last of the tunnels. You are all covered with mud. You find yourselves in a wide, underground chamber, the floor of which is covered with circular pools of water. Each of these is surrounded by a low rim of rock, making them look like a collection of large bowls.

Then, on the far side of the chamber, you see a group of people all huddled together and looking in your direction. There are expressions of fear on their faces.

"Those must be the refugees that Fendar and Vankon were talking about," you say.

You raise your arms in what you mean to be a sign of peace. This only seems to frighten the refugees more.

"We are friends of Fendar and Vankon," you call out. "We are here to help you."

There is a confused murmuring among the refugees, but they still seem afraid.

"Look at us," Aran says to you. "If creatures looking like us came out of the walls, we'd be frightened too. Let's wash off in one of these pools. Then they can see what we really look like."

"Good idea," says Teppin. "Frankly, I could use a bath after those slimy tunnels."

All three of you slip into one of the pools and splash around until all the mud has been washed off. Then you sit on the rim of the pool and wait. One of the refugees, an old man with a long, white beard comes over to you.

"Forgive us for being afraid," he says, "but we thought that you were some of the mud people. They sometimes come here to attack us."

"You mean there are people living in those tunnels?" you say.

Go to next page.

"You were lucky to get through," says the old man. "Even the zarks are afraid of them. That's one reason that we chose this place for our refuge, even though we had to come through the mud tunnels ourselves to get here. We lost many on the way."

"I was wondering why the zarks didn't come after us," you say.

"So you see," says the old man, "we are trapped here, living on the few fish that grow in the shallow ponds, one of which you—"

"Sorry about that," you say, "but it was the only way that we could get rid of the mud."

"I know," says the old man. "It's all right. By the way, my name is Travan. I guess you are trapped here now the way we are."

"But we have to get through to the vords to see if the antidote that Vankon gave us works."

"I'm sorry," Travan says, "but there's no—"

He is interrupted by a small boy pulling at his sleeve.

"Yes, Tlon, what is it?" Travan asks.

"I know a tunnel that no one else knows," Tlon says. "Vana and I found it playing at the far end of the cavern. We were crawling in one of those deep holes there

and . . ."

"Shame on you," Travan says. "You know that you're not supposed to go into those holes."

"But grandad, this hole went on and on. We went in a long way, until we got scared and came back," Tlon says.

"Very well," Travan says. "At least you spoke up. You may have discovered something very useful."

"Do you think that this tunnel might get us into Sline's territory?" Teppin asks.

"I don't know that it goes anywhere," Travan says. "As you know, it's the first I've heard of it. If it does lead to the 'city of terror,' it might also lead the zarks back here."

"City of terror!" you exclaim.

"That's what we call the huge city that Sline is building. He's using the vords as slave labor with the zorks as guards and overseers. When the city is finished, he plans to make it the capital of an underground empire—an empire that he plans to spread to the surface. he has dreams of conquering the whole world."

"Then the time to stop him is now," says Teppin. "Let's give Tlon's tunnel a try."

Before you go, the refugees serve you all a meal of fish and mushrooms. Some of them beg you not to go, but others congratulate you on your bravery. Finally, Tlon guides you to the tunnel he had found at the far end of the cavern. You thank him and go into the tunnel. It is very narrow and cramped for awhile, then it opens up into a series of chambers, some of interconnected and some not.

Go to next page.

Find your way through this new labyrinth. But be careful. Hidden dangers may lurk in its many chambers.

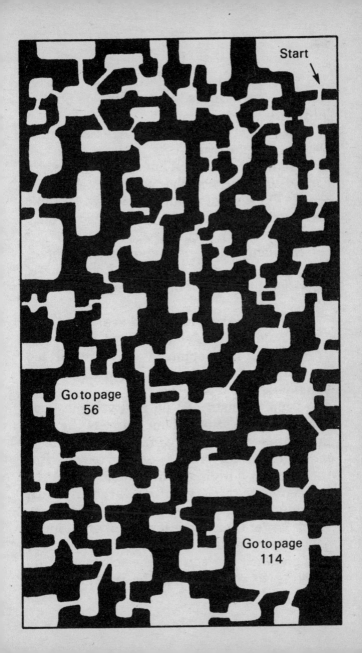

You, Teppin, and Aran plod on and on through the hundreds of chambers in the labyrinth.

"We're getting nowhere!" Aran exclaims, as you stop to rest.

"I know," you say, "but these rooms were carved out by somebody at sometime or other. They must lead somewhere. I can't believe that the refugee cavern has the only entrance into this complex."

Suddenly, there is a shout from Teppin, peering into the next chamber. "Look in here! There's a bright spot of light high up on the wall."

You and Aran run in to see.

"Could it be daylight?" you ask.

"I doubt it," Teppin says, "we're still too far underground. Here, stand on my shoulders and take a look."

Teppin hoists you up and you put your eye to the hole. Spread out below is the vast panorama of a huge cavern. It's almost like a mountain valley on the surface, except that the "sky" is a high, arching dome of rock. In the center of the cavern is a large city with buildings and streets. One of the buildings is much larger than the rest and only half-built. You guess that this is Sline's palace. Even at this distance you can see the scores of vords working to complete it. The interior of the cavern is illuminated by the hundreds of torches burning in the city.

You climb down and give Aran a turn. Then both you and Aran support Teppin so that he can see.

"I'd like to get down there and try out the antidote on some of those vords," Teppin says.

"There's no way we can get through that small hole," Aran says.

Go to next page.

"Maybe we can open it up a little," Teppin says, reaching into the hole with his hand and pulling a rock loose. "I think this *was* a larger opening once. Then it was sealed up."

Teppin is heavy, but you and Aran somehow manage to hold him up there while he starts pulling rocks loose and tossing them back into the chamber. Soon the hole is noticeably larger.

Then, Teppin jumps down from your shoulders.

"We'll take turns," he says.

Aran climbs up next. Then finally, you take your turn pulliing the rocks loose.

"I think the hole is large enough now," you call down. "I'm going to poke my head through."

Just outside the hole there's a drop of about fifteen feet down to a narrow rock ledge. Then another drop from there of another two hundred feet, down to the floor of the underground valley. The ledge extends way to the right where the face of the cliff seems jagged enough to climb.

"Hold the end of my whip," you say. "I'm going to use it to slide down to that ledge."

After you get there, Aran follows. Then Teppin, after first tossing your whip to you, climbs out and hangs down as far as he can.

He drops the remaining distance to the ledge. You and Aran manage to break his fall by grabbing him from both sides.

"I hope nobody's looking this way just now," you say.

"Don't worry," Teppin says. "We're in deep shadow as far as anyone down there is concerned."

"Still, we'd better be very careful," Aran says. "I can make out, even from this distance, what looks like a lot of zarks in that city."

Go to next page.

You all carefully make your way down the face of the cliff. Fortunately, at the bottom, there are a lot of rock formations between you and the city. You keep to the shadows and creep closer and closer.

Then suddenly, you see a group of zarks heading your way. For a moment, you think that you've been spotted. You all get set to make a run for it back to the cliff. but then you realize that they are heading for the city. They are leading a group of prisoners, their hands tied behind their backs. And one of the prisoners is Prince Fendar!

"Looks like they captured Fendar," Teppin says.

"That's terrible," says Aran. "We've got to do something."

"You're right," you say. "We can't let them turn Fendar into a vord."

"There are only four zarks and half a dozen prisoners," Teppin says. "And the prisoners aren't vords. If we jump the zarks, the prisoners can help us. We can get away before the zarks realize what's happened."

"Get away to where?" you ask.

"I don't know," Teppin says. "Back to the cliff, I guess. But we can decide that after we rescue Fendar. Maybe he has some ideas."

"OK, here they come," you whisper. "I'll

take the one in front."

The zarks with their prisoners pass in front of the rock where you are hiding. Aran topples the two rear guards with quick shots from his slingshot. Teppin jumps out and drops one of the guards in front with a roundhouse blow to the jaw. Your whip wraps around the throat of the last one, yanking him to the ground. As this last one tries to get up, Teppin knocks him unconscious with a blow from his knee. Then Teppin quickly cuts the prisoners loose with his knife.

Go to next page.

"Let's get back to the cliff!" Teppin shouts.

Unfortunately, a shout of alarm goes up from the zark guards on the nearby buildings. Dozens of zarks come pouring out. You all run as fast as you can away from the city. But the zarks know the valley and its rocks a lot better than you do, and soon you are surrounded. You put up a good fight but there are too many of them. Soon they have you subdued and tied up.

"Good try," you say to your friends as the zarks lead you toward the partially completed palace. "We were just outnumbered."

"Thanks for trying," says Fendar, being herded along beside you. "I really appreciate it."

"Let's don't give up yet," Teppin whispers." "I have a plan."

"I hope it's a good one," Aran says.

You are led into the palace and then across a vast throne room. At the other side, at the top of a high stairway, is Sline himself sitting on his throne and glaring angrily down at you.

"So, what have we here?" he snarls. "Creatures from the upper world, to gauge from your darkened skins. Very good. You will be the first of your kind to, shall we say, serve the great Emperor Sline. And you came to

help Prince—I should say ex-Prince—Fendar. How nice. Well you can help him slave to build my palace. Bring the trope."

A zark comes from behind the throne carrying a goblet full of a dark liquid.

"Now if you will be my guest," Sline says with a smirk, "and take a sip or two...."

"Aha! Well, I am a bit thirsty," says Teppin. "Perhaps I should go first."

"By all means," says Sline, directing the zark with the goblet towards Teppin.

"What do you think you're doing?" you whisper to Teppin.

"I have some of the antidote powder hidden in my palm," Teppin whispers back. "I'll slip it into the trope before I drink it. I just hope it works. Remember, pretend we're vords after...."

Teppin takes a long look at the trope before drinking, pretending to admire it. "Tasty looking liquid, I must say," he says, shaking it around in the goblet.

"Enough of that," orders Sline. "Let's get on with it."

Teppin takes a swallow, then passes the goblet to you. You take a drink then pass it on to Aran who does the same. The liquid tastes sweet, but it has a bitter aftertaste.

Almost immediately, you start to feel dizzy. Your vision clouds over, and strange forms seem to swim around you. You know that it's the trope trying to capture your mind. But you also feel somehow that the antidote is working. The forms swirling in front of your eyes are forming a maze—a maze that you have to get through to avoid becoming a vord.

Go to next page.

Find your way through the trope maze. Be careful or you may really end up as a vord.

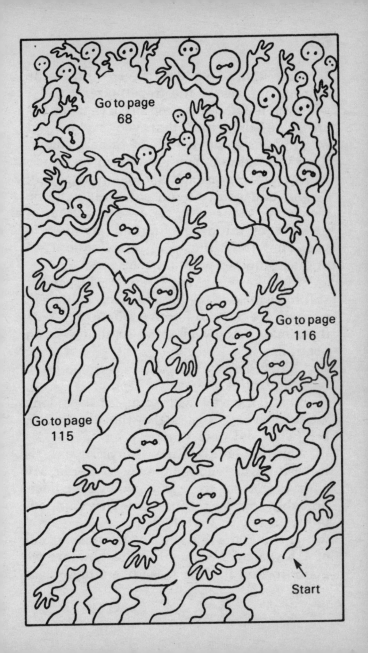

Go to page
68

Go to page
116

Go to page
115

Start

You seem to wander forever through the swirling images of the trope maze. Finally, you seem to fall into a deep sleep. In it you are dreaming—dreaming that you are a vord working on a stone wall of Sline's palace. Then you wake up. You *are* working on Sline's palace. But you are not a vord—you know it. Teppin and Aran are on either side of you, also laying stones. Not far away is a group of zarks. They are not paying any attention to you. They think that you, Teppin, and Aran are just another work crew of vords.

"Just keep working," Teppin whispers. "I still have most of the antidote tucked away in my belt. We have to find out where they keep their main supply of trope so that we can neutralize it."

"They got my slingshot," Aran says.

"And my knife," says Teppin.

"I still have my whip wrapped around my waist," you say. "I guess they thought it was a belt. They did take Vankon's light."

Our best bet right now," says Teppin, "is to keep on pretending that we're vords. My guess is that the trope is stored in the palace, probably near the throne room. They came out pretty fast with that goblet."

"I think you're right," Aran whispers out of the side of his mouth. "But how are we going to find it. This looks like a big palace even though it's unfinished. There must be a maze of halls, rooms, and corridors inside."

"We'll find the trope somehow," Teppin says. "The problem now is getting into the palace without the zarks getting suspicious."

"We can pretend that we have to carry some of these rocks inside to finish the other side of the wall," you whisper.

"Might work," Teppin whispers back. "Make your motions look as mechanical as possible."

You each pick up a rock, and, like a file of zombies, march around the wall and into the palace. Once the wall is between you and the zarks, you stop and listen. The zarks don't seem to have noticed your marching away.

"The guards are probably so used to the vords behaving like good slaves, that they didn't think anything strange about our coming in here," Aran says.

"Still, we'd better be careful," Teppin says. "All of the vords may not be that lazy."

You all put down the rocks and start into the many rooms and corridors of the palace.

Go to next page.

Find your way through the palace maze to where Sline keeps his main supply of trope. But be careful. The zarks are all around you.

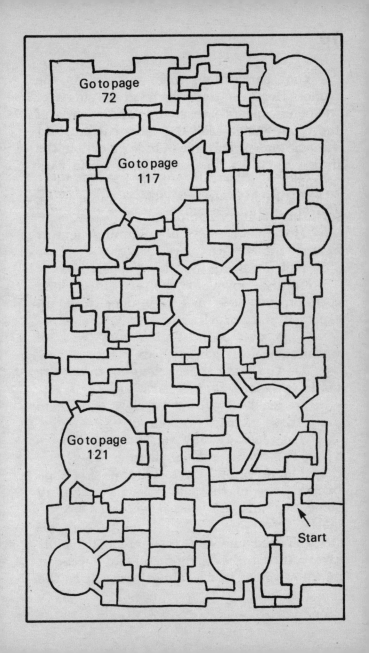

You search from room to room in the palace. Some of them have great stores of weapons—spears, crossbows, and swords of the types you've seen the zarks carrying. At various times, you have to hide quickly in the dark corners of the corridors to avoid zark patrols.

"Looks like Sline is storing up weapons for a big military campaign," you say.

"He must *really* be planning a war against the surface," Aran says.

"Not if we can stop it," Teppin says.

Finally, down at the end of a long corridor, you see a heavy door with an especially large zark guard on each side.

"This could be it," Teppin says. "Now all we have to do is get in there."

"Do you think that pretending that we're vords will work again?" Aran asks.

"At least it will get us close enough to jump those guards," Teppin says.

"They look awfully big," you say. "We're going to have a problem there."

"You're right," says Teppin. "Let's go back to one of those storerooms and grab some weapons. At least it will even up the odds."

You find one of the storerooms not far away. Aran grabs a long metal bar, a weapon he knows how to use almost as well as the

slingshot. Teppin finds a short sword, close enough in size to his long knife to make him feel comfortable with it.

Then you all go back toward the guarded door. You march along mechanically holding your weapons behind you. The guards by the door don't bat an eye until you are right on top of them. They are taken completely by surprise. Aran takes the one on the left, jabbing him first in the stomach with his bar, making the guard double over. Then he raps him over the head, knocking him cold. Your whip wraps around the other guard's neck, pulling him down to where Teppin can conk him on the head with the flat of his sword.

"Quick! Through the door!" Teppin shouts.

there are no more guards inside the room. But there are two large vats filled with trope. Teppin runs over and divides the antidote powder between them. "Now, let's get out of here fast," he says.

But just as you are about to go back out of the door, you hear the heavy tread of a zark patrol coming down the corridor and then angry shouts as they discover their unconscious comrades. They dash into the room. You, Teppin, and Aran run back behind the vats, preparing to defend yourselves.

"Look!" says Aran. "Some kind of very

large tubing ends here. It could be part of the equipment for making the trope. It might also be a way to escape."

"You're right," Teppin says. "It's large enough to crawl through."

You lead the way into the tubing. Teppin and Aran follow. When you are in a ways, the tubing gets larger, but you still can't fully stand up, but at least you can move more quickly running in a crouch. The tubing starts dividing into different channels and turns into a confusing maze.

Find your way through the tubing maze.

Go to page
124

Go to page
78

Go to page
122

Start

You come out of the tubing maze into a room filled with equipment similar to that in Vankon's cave. There is a guard dozing just inside of a bolted door on the far side. He is the only one in the room. He wakes up with a start, then he tries to unbolt the door. Teppin dashes across the room and stops him, holding him at swordpoint until you can tie him up.

It's a good thing you managed to stop the guard from unlocking the door. Almost immediately a loud pounding begins on the other side of it. As thick as the door is, you can hear the angry shouts coming from beyond.

"It sounds like all the zarks in the underground kingdom are out there," Aran says.

"What'll we do now?" you say. "The only other way out of here seems to be through the tubing, and there are plenty of zarks at the other end."

"I don't care how many zarks there are," Teppin says. "We'll give them a good fight this time."

"We may not have to," Aran says. "I have an idea. You remember that illusion maze that the young sorcerer, Warkus, used to help us escape in the Castle of Doom adventure. Well, he taught the magic formula to me. I'm going to try it."

what you can with your whip. Soon the trope
factory is in a shambles. And none too soon.
There is a crash as the door gives way and
topples into the room. The zarks spring in. But
they are wary. They know that you and your

friends are no pushovers.

Aran quickly chants the syllables that Warkus had taught him, and he makes a diagram in the air with his hand. Then, just as the zarks attack, you, Teppin, and Aran fade from their view.

Find your way through the illusion maze. But be careful. You never know where you are going to end up with this kind of maze.

Go to page 84

Go to page 127

Go to page 125

Start →

You come out of the illusion maze into a terrifying scene. There are red-hot walls and columns of flame all around you. You, Teppin, and Aran find yourselves on a narrow ledge high above a bubbling stream of molten rock. It's like being in an oven.

"Wow!" Aran exclaims. "Maybe we should have stayed and fought the zarks."

Go to next page.

"We must be very deep in the earth," Teppin says. "I've heard that the deeper you go down, the hotter it gets."

You hear a scurrying above you. As you look up, you see on an upper ledge, a number of red creatures with pointed ears and long tails that end in barbs. When you look at them, they seem to vanish. Teppin sees them too.

"The fact that there are creatures down here," he says, "means that there's a way in *and* a way out. This ledge we're on goes upward. Let's follow it."

You go along the ledge for awhile. It is definitely getting less hot as you go up. But not much. And the heat is beginning to have its effect on you. You feel dizzy and weak. Every once in a while you see some of the red creatures poke their long, pointed faces out of a glowing crevice above or below you. Fortuantely, the ledge you are following doesn't seem to be as hot as the rest of the fiery cavern, though the heat of the rock is coming through your sandals and burning your feet. The wall beside you is still painfully hot to the touch.

"We'd better get somewhere cooler soon," Aran gasps, "or we're going to be cooked."

"Don't give up now," Teppin says. "I think I see a change in the wall by the ledge up ahead. It doesn't look as hot."

You get there just in time. You couldn't have gone much further. The ledge widens and goes through an archway becoming a tunnel. The tunnel then turns into a maze. It's still very hot inside it. But at least it's bearable.

Go to next page.

Find your way through the hot maze.

Go to page 90

Go to page 126

Start

You've made it through the hot maze. you all sit down on the floor to rest.

"I'm glad to be out of there," you say. "That was the worst."

"More dangers lie ahead of us, I suspect," Teppin says, "but I think we've gotten through one of the most dangerous."

After resting for a few hours, you start off again. You come to a large metal door, the surface of which is sculptured with hundreds of grotesque faces. You recognize many of them as those of zarks. The door itself is tightly bolted on the other side. At the bottom is a large sculptured head with a gaping mouth. You can see through the mouth to the other side of the door, and it looks large enought to crawl through. But there are rows of sharp teeth on the top and the bottom.

Teppin peers through the opening, then carefully feels around inside. Suddenly, he jerks his arm back as a mechanism is released inside the mouth and the teeth come clashing together. Then they snap open again.

"Somebody crawling through there would have been cut in two," Teppin says.

"What are we going to do?" Aran asks.

"I have an idea," Teppin says, pulling the sword he took from the palace out of his belt. He reaches into the mouth and wedges the sword between the upper and lower rows of teeth. Then he trips the mechanism again. There is a groan of metal and a grinding sound, but the sword keeps the jaws from closing.

"I think we can get through now," Teppin says, "but we still have to find a way of crawling over those teeth without cutting ourselves."

"Maybe I can dull them a bit," Aran says. "At least the ones on the bottom."

Aran wades in with his metal bar, whacking away at the teeth. The metal of the teeth is fairly soft. Soon the points are dulled or bent over.

"That did it!" you exclaim.

Teppin crawls through first. Then you and Aran follow.

Go to next page.

On the other side of the door is a large room, and beyond that is the entrance to another tunnel. You all cross the room and cautiously go in. Along both sides of it are rows of square wooden benches. And on top of each bench is a sleeping zark.

"This is where the zarks must hibernate," Teppin says. "I suspect that Sline has revived only a part of them with his trope. He probably plans to revive all of them for his attack on the surface."

"I think we've put a dent in those plans," you say.

"Right," says Teppin. "But we don't know how long it will take him to get his trope-making apparatus back in operation."

"Maybe all of the vords will come out of their stupor and all of the zarks will go back to sleep before he does," you say.

"I hope so," says Teppin, "but we can't be sure, Right now let's see where these hibernation tunnels lead."

Go to next page.

Find your way through the hibernation tunnels. But be careful. All of the zarks down there may not be hibernating.

Go to page
96

Go to page
118

Start

Suddenly, you turn a corner in the hibernation maze and see a long column of wide awake zarks heading toward you. At least they appear to be wide awake at first. Then you notice that they all have a kind of glazed look in their eyes. They file right past, never even noticing you. They are all on their

way back to hibernation.

Cautiously, you move forward into another room. From the room just beyond that one you hear angry shouting. An argument is going on. You immediately recognize one of the voices as Sline's.

"Can I help it if some meddling fools from

the surface destroyed my equipment," he shouts.

"Excuses, excuses!" the other voice shouts back. "You have betrayed us. All of my troops are going back into hibernation. Without the trope I can't stop myself from doing the same."

"I promise you," Sline says, "that when you come out of hibernation the next time, all will be ready, General Zabar, for the attack on the surface and—"

"I'll *be* out of hibernation again all right," Zabar interrupts, "but *you* won't be around to see it."

You hear a scream from Sline and a swishing sound. Then silence. Zabar, bloody sword in hand, stumbles sleepily past you heading for his hibernation bench.

You, Teppin, and Aran go on down the now spacious corridor. Up ahead is a wide stairway going upward. You climb up it and emerge on the surface of the subterranean valley.

All around you, people are celebrating wildly. All the vords have been freed. When they see you, a tremendous cheer goes up. Prince Fendar comes running over, his eyes wet with joy.

"My friends, you have saved us all," he exclaims. "We owe you everything. Name your reward—anything!"

"Thanks, Fendar, but what we'd like most right now is just to get back to our ship. If you could show us the way...."

There is a sudden silence.

Go to next page.

"We would certainly like to see you get back to the surface, if that's what you wish," Fendar says. "But I'm afraid that the tunnels through which I brought you here have all collapsed."

Fendar sinks into thought. Then a familiar, high-pitched voice comes out of the crowd. It's the alchemist, Vankon!

"There is a way. There's a path through the once fiery mountain. It will lead you to the surface... at least I think it will," he says.

"Great!" exclaims Fendar. "And I'll go with you to make sure you get there."

"No Fendar," you say. "Your place is here with your people."

Fendar, however, refuses to let you go right away. He insists that you stay for a week of festivities. By the end of the week, you are so tired of constant praise, that you are more than anxious to get going. Vankon leads you to the far end of the valley then through a long tunnel to a shaft leading straight up.

"This is the path to the surface?" you ask.

"I didn't say it was going to be easy," Vankon says.

"Well, it's all we have," Teppin says. "We'll make it somehow."

"Thanks, Vankon, for bringing us here," you say. "And I haven't forgotten that your making the antidote to Sline's poison was as important in freeing your people as what we did."

You wave farewell to Vankon and start up the shaft. This shaft leads to another shaft and soon it turns into a maze. But as Teppin just said, it's all you've got.

Go to next page.

Find your way through the mountain maze.

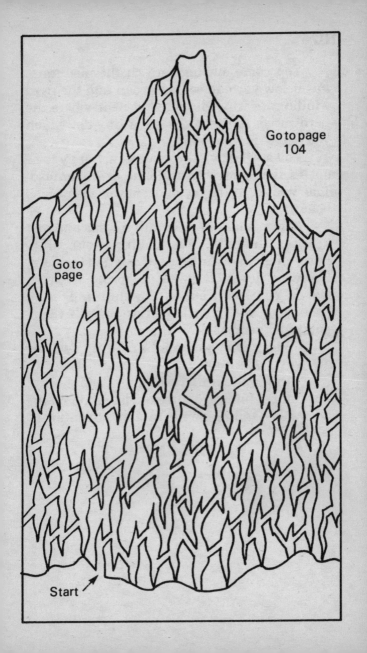

Go to page 104

Go to page

Start

You come out high up on the mountain. Far below you can see the ocean and the fjord winding its way inland. And near where the fjord meets the sea, you see a tiny dot which you know is your ship.

You start down the mountain, happy to be out in the open with the blue sky overhead. The white, cottony clouds never seemed so beautiful.

A few hours of downhill hiking and you are on the cliff overlooking your ship. Fortunately, you find a path down to the fjord. Halfway down, there is a spring of fresh water. You swim out to the ship and bring back your water casks. After you fill them, you pull them back to the ship.

"Well, we got our drinking water, anyway," Aran says.

"*And*, quite an adventure," Teppin adds.

Sunset finds the three of you again on the open sea—sailing south to new adventures.

THE END

While your attention has momentarily been on the boy pulled from the water, the ship has drifted closer to the center of the whirlpool. As soon as you realize what's happening, you try to steer the other way. But this only makes things worse. It's as though a giant, invisible hand is pulling the ship toward the deadly vortex, which yawns like a huge, terrible mouth ready to gobble you up.

The ship spins around—faster and faster—as you are pulled into the vortex itself. Suddenly, you find yourself falling into the very center of the whirlpool. The ship spins around for a moment like a top, and then vanishes—you with it—into the depths of the sea.

THE END

If you don't like this ending, go back to page 12 and try again.

You search through the cavern for what seems like forever. Finally, you all sink exhausted to the floor. For a while, the only sounds are those of your breathing and the faint plop of water from the high ceiling. Then you begin to hear rustlings in the darkness all around you. At first you can't see anything in the dim light. But dark, menacing shapes begin to take form on all sides. You, Teppin, and Aran jump to your feet—just as a hail of spears and arrows comes flying through the darkness. You sink back to the floor, a dozen arrows in your back.

THE END

If you don't like this ending, go back to page 26 and try again.

Carefully you work your way through the jagged maze. You are glad that you have the light that Vankon gave you. The jagged edges of the rocks are razor sharp. If you so much as touch one accidentally, you get a nasty cut.

As you go along, you keep hearing faint, grinding sounds. It's as though the rocks in the tunnel were moving slightly. Then the sounds start to get louder and louder. They are all around you now. As you approach one of the sharp stones it seems to move slightly—as if your coming toward it activated some mechanism in the wall.

The stones start to move faster and faster. Some of them move to block your way through the tunnels. As the passageway directly in front of you is blocked, you turn to go in the other direction. But another stone cuts you off. You are trapped in the tight space between the two.

Then, you realize to your horror, that another of the sharp blades of stone is moving toward you from the side. You try to squeeze out of its way, but there's not enough room. The sharp blade slowly cuts you in two.

THE END

If you don't like this ending, go back to page 36 and try again.

You, Teppin, and Aran keep going on and on through the passageways. Every once in a while there is a tremor beneath your feet.

"I sure hope that shaking doesn't get any worse," you say. "Those rock spears on the ceiling could break loose and fall on our heads."

Then suddenly, as if the ground were mocking what you just said, there is a tremendous jolt that knocks you all to the ground. A terrible rumbling sound roars through the cavern. The stone spears *do* start to break loose and crash down around you.

"Quick!" Teppin shouts, struggling to his feet. "We've got to get out of this part of the cavern."

You all struggle forward with the ground shaking violently under you. But you don't get very far. The whole ceiling above you breaks loose and crashes down—burying you under tons of rock.

THE END

If you don't like this ending, go back to page 26 and try again.

You all slosh your way through the tunnels of wet mud. In some places the floor is so soft that you sink in up to your ankles. The heavy mud sticks to your feet and makes it an effort to walk. But somehow you keep going. Once, when you stop to rest, you lean against the wall for support and your arm sinks to your elbow in the gooey mess.

Then you start to hear a gurgling sound. The mud begins to bubble up behind you. The walls themselves are now sagging down and inward as though they are about to become liquid and flow down into the tunnel. A few minutes later this is what does happen. Suddenly, you find yourselves up to your waists in the liquid mud. Then the tunnel fills up completely with the stuff, drowning your all in the thick ooze.

THE END

If you don't like this ending, go back to page 46 and try again.

You struggle through the passageways surrounded by the soft mud. Your feet sink in and want to stick to the floor. It's like wading through molasses.

Then, you come to large room. The floor, walls and ceiling are still made of mud, but along the walls you see the outlines of several giant creatures. You realize with horror that they are coming right out of the walls. Suddenly, they are all around you, blocking your escape back into the smaller passageways. One of them snatches you up, and with tremendous force hurles you head first into the mud wall of the chamber. You sink in up to your waist. You find yourself held fast by the suffocating grip of the mud. Your legs, the only part of you still free, thrash around for a bit—but not for long.

THE END

If you don't like this ending, go back to page 46 and try again.

You, Teppin, and Aran search through one room after another. Somethimes the room is a dead end, other times it has another door which leads into a new corridor to still another room.

You are investigating one of these, when you hear a click behind you. You turn to see a door slowly sliding out of the wall. All of you rush out of the room just in time to escape being sealed in.

You go on through more rooms, but now you are all on your guard against more closing doors. Finally, you all stop to rest in one of the rooms. You sit down wearily on the floor, your backs against the wall. Suddenly, there are clicks on both sides of the room. You jump up as fast as you can, but this time doors on each side quickly slide shut. You are sealed in.

For hours, you push and bang on the solid doors. You look frantically for hidden switches that will reopen them. You can't find any. You keep on searching until all the oxygen in the room has been used up, and you slump lifeless to the floor.

THE END

If you don't like this ending, go back to
page 54 and try again.

You fight your way through the swirling forms and strange creatures. At each turn in the maze, they threaten to gobble you up. You do the best you can, but your mind is confused—you can't tell which way is up and which way is down. Somewhere you make a wrong move. Several of the creatures wrap around you. Their tentacles have you in an iron grip that gets tighter and tighter—and tighter! Your bones begin to snap. Soon all of the life is squeezed out of you.

THE END

If you don't like this ending, turn to page 66 and try again.

You try your best to get through the maze, but everything is a blur. The trope creatures are after you from the start. They seem to block your way everywhere you turn. Then, one of them wraps around your head and starts to pull the top of it off. You try to stop it, but another one grabs your arms and pins them behind your back. The creature on your head is now pulling out your brain and replacing it with—itself!

Suddenly, you are back in the throne room. Your only thoughts are to serve and obey your lord and master, Sline. You are now a perfect vord.

THE END

If you don't like this ending, go back to page 66 and try again.

You search through the palace. You keep to the shadows the best you can. The palace is full of zork patrols. You are halfway down one of the corridors when you hear the heavy tramp of a patrol coming toward you. You all rush back down the corridor looking for a way to escape. Unfortunately, you come to a large, tightly locked door. You struggle to get it open before the zorks arrive.

But it's no use, the zorks trap you there against the door. You immediately pretend to be vords and try to march away.

"Don't you know that this section of the palace is off limits to vords?" bellows the commander of the patrol. "Any vords found here are to be killed immediately."

You start to protest, but a volley of arrows from the zorks stops you short.

THE END

If you don't like this ending, go back to page 70 and try again.

Carefully, you work your way through the maze. All of the zarks there seem to be sleeping peacefully, but you can never be

sure. Up ahead you see what you think is the
exit from the maze. But just before you get
there, the zarks by the door rise up and,

grabbing their weapons, come toward you. You try to retreat, but more of the zarks rise up behind you.

Then, they charge, their swords slashing away. You fight bravely, but there are too many of them. They cut you to pieces. Then the zorks quietly return to their benches and go back to sleep.

THE END

If you don't like this ending, go back to page 94 and try again.

You search through the palace, keeping to the shadows and what appear to be little-used corridors. You sneak through a small door into a large, very dark space.

"This could be where they keep the trope," you say. "I wish they hadn't taken Vankon's light away from me. I can't see a thing."

Suddenly, the space you are in lights up as torches blaze into life all around the hall. Somehow, you've found your way back to the throne room. Sline is sitting above you on his throne.

"So you somehow defeated the trope," he snarls, "but you won't escape this."

Sline raises his arm as a signal, and suddenly a trap door opens up beneath you. You tumble into a deep pit full of snakes—poisonous ones.

THE END

If you don't like this ending, go back to page 70 and try again.

You hurry through the large tubing. You are about halfway through the confusing maze, when you hear the ominous sound of rushing water. But, it isn't water, it's trope and it's rushing toward you. You all run back the other way, but before you can get very far, the wave of trope hits you. You all go under the fluid as you are washed along. At first, you manage to keep from swallowing any of the trope. You don't want to become a vord. Then, as you begin to lose consciousness in the fluid, you realize that you won't live long enough to become one.

THE END

If you don't like this ending, go back to page 76 and try again.

You, Teppin, and Aran climb up and up the steep, almost vertical side of the wide shaft. Towards the top, the going gets really rough. There are fewer and fewer places to grip the rock. Finally, you struggle to the top of a tall pinnacle. There is just enough room at the top for three of you to stop and rest.

You are about to start climbing again, when you feel the whole column of rock shift under you. Then, before you can jump free, it slides off the side of the shaft and goes crashing—with you on it—to the bottom of the crevice hundreds of feet below.

THE END

If you don't like this ending, go back to page 102 and try again.

You rush through the tubing. Suddenly, you come to where it's plugged. You go back the other way, only to find that that way now is blocked too.

Then the two plugs that you are trapped between start to move toward you. You, Teppin, and Aran use all of your strength to hold them off, but it's no use. You are finally crushed between them.

THE END

If you don't like this ending, go back to page 76 and try again.

At the moment you start to rematerialize from the illusion maze, you realize that there is something terribly wrong. You re-enter in a small hollow in the rock far beneath the earth. You don't know where your friends are, but you suspect that they are also trapped in the rock not far away.

You don't know how you know, but you realize to your horror that there are hundreds of feet of solid rock over you. Quickly, you recite the magic syllables that Warkus taught you—to try to throw you back into the illusion maze. But, it's no use. Without the hand gestures the spell will not work—and you are so tightly squeezed into the rock that you can hardly move a muscle.

THE END

If you don't like this ending, go back to page 82 and try again.

You struggle through the intense heat in the maze. Then, you turn one of the corners in the tunnel and find there ahead of you a row of big, red creatures with barbed tails. They are spitting and snarling. Another group of them suddenly appears behind you. Without warning, both groups attack. You manage to fight them off for awhile, but the more of them you knock down, the more seem to appear. The barbs in their tails are razor sharp and deadly. You don't last long.

THE END

If you don't like this ending, go back to page 88 and try again.

Unfortunately, the hard thing to control with an illusion maze is where you re-enter. This time you re-enter in the air high above a lake of molten rock. As you start to rematerialize from the illusion maze, you hang there for a few moments, looking down in terror at the fiery pool below. Then, at the moment that you are fully materialized, you drop like a stone—straight down into the molten rock.

THE END

If you don't like this ending, go back to page 82 and try again.

In the YOUR **AMAZING** adventures™ series, each book contains a new quest, new obstacles to be overcome, new mazes, and new dangers. And don't forget, *you* are the hero or heroine.

Now in print: